A S

A C

MW01602204

PUBLISHED BY

New World Theatre Publishing
Londonderry, NH

A SOLITARY VOICE

TABLE OF CONTENTS

FOREWORD

There is a paradoxical moment unique to the stage when a single actor speaking in a solitary voice is the momentary center of a complex narrative universe. A fragile, tenuous, and compelling bond forms as the spoken words command the focus of every eye and every ear sharing in the telling and receiving of a story. A character speaks a monologue or a soliloquy as part of a larger story or as the story itself and for the briefest of times the art of the playwright, the heart of the character, and the craft of the actor connect to the individual id and collective ego of the audience in a manner that resonates in a moment that is unique every time it plays. Be it Macbeth contemplating all that he has lost and all that he will lose in this life and the next if what is done cannot be undone tomorrow and tomorrow and tomorrow or Hamlet considering what dreams may come, this quintessence of dust does not exist in the passive viewing of a film, or in the reader's internal voice narrating the page, or the emotive cues of music. It is a synchronous experience in which the music of the spoken word consorts with the strings of the heart in an aspect that is simultaneously shared universally and experienced individually.

The paradox is that the solitary voice is, in reality, many voices speaking as one. It is a piece in which each individual in the experience is, in part, an author. It is the playwright articulating as the character in response to the narrative through the interpretation of an actor into the personal zeitgeist of the audience. It is so delicate that almost any subtle internal or external change affects it. It can always exist but it can never be the same twice. Consider the nuance when Henry V's rousing patriotic speeches rally a nation bracing for war or pluck at the heartstrings of a veteran weary of combat, sacrifice, and loss. To write, speak, or receive the solitary voice is to be part of the narrative.

In that sense, New World Theatre is proud to present A Solitary Voice, a collection that celebrates the art and craft of many voices speaking as one. Regrettably, this volume does not contain all the talent available to us and in that regard we thank the many talented authors whose works grace these pages as well as those whose works were submitted but were unable to be included. May center stage bless all of your dramatic endeavors. And to the actors who may speak these words and audiences who may bring their own narratives to the theater to shape them, we welcome you to enjoy these solitary voices speaking in unison with your own.

Walter A. Freeman

Playwright
New World Theatre
Playwrights' Collective

PERFORMANCE RIGHTS

Performance rights and royalty license agreements must be obtained when any of the works within this anthology are performed before a paying audience.

For those seeking to perform all the monologues within this collection, contact New World Theatre to obtain a royalty license agreement for *A Solitary Voice*.

For those seeking to perform one or more of the monologues within this collection, but not all of them, contact the individual playwright to obtain a royalty license agreement.

All playwright contact information is available in APPENDIX B of this anthology.

SPLAT

By Erica Furgiuele
(From "Protocol", a full-length play)

Harry walks on, carrying a bottle of pills. He arrives center stage, stops, takes two tablets from the bottle, pops them in his mouth, and swallows them. He addresses the audience.

HARRY: Do you remember the fifth grade egg-drop project? Where your teacher, who also happens to be the baseball coach, hurls your cobbled-together contraption off the school roof? And you think, just for a moment, you're invincible. The ground falls away, and all you're left with is flight. The feeling that somehow, you're gonna make it.

He takes a pill.

But then, splat. Physics once again proves that yes, eggs break from a height of two feet let alone 30.

Another pill.

And all that trouble you went to protecting the egg from its demise was simply a waste of time. And where you could have 20 cute, fluffy baby chicks, you have a parking lot full of egg drop soup. That always got me.

Another pill.

I suspended mine in honey. "A+." But you can't suspend human beings in honey, at least not without several calls from the neighbors and the landlord and your therapist.

Another pill.

And that's life. One beautiful but deadly mathematical curve towards oblivion. Some of us have enough padding for the fall, and others don't.

Another pill.

Man, I should have been a poet. But I gave it up for my real love, auditing. I just do limericks on the side sometimes.

Another pill.

It's like someone is constantly running their nails along a chalkboard, except that chalkboard is underneath my skin. And that someone...

Another pill.

Tears and slamming doors aren't the problem. Your well-meaning yet slightly psychotic entourage is not the problem. It's the absence of those things. The vacuum. The infinities between words, between heartbeats. Because all we have is mortality. The rest is fabrication.

Another pill.

Human resourcefulness, however boundless, can never compensate for our sheer fragility. Fingers snap like baby carrots, flesh melts in flame, veins open and we succumb.

Another pill.

Isn't that just beautiful? That the body, despite all of our poking and prodding and squeezing and cleansing, can still triumph over the mind? Sure, the egg looks undamaged on the outside, but is it really?

Another pill.

Eventually, we all end up splat on the pavement in one way or another. And life is just that agonizing, horrifying, spellbinding thirty-foot drop to the ground.

It's over before you can blink.

Pause, another pill.

It's over before you can say, "boo." It's over before it even begins.

THE LOOK

By Greg Hovanesian

At rise the SCREENWRITER/PLAYWRIGHT, a man in his 20s or 30s, sits at a desk. A script lies in front of him. He wears cool-looking jeans, maybe some rips in them, and a cool and interesting T-shirt. Maybe he has a pencil behind his ears. The SCREENWRITER /PLAYWRIGHT appears to be talking to another person sitting nearby, but the audience never sees him or her.

SCREENWRITER/PLAYWRIGHT: Three words. That's it. That's all he said. Three words.

>   *Pointing at the script in front of him.*

'You see this?'

That's it. That's all he said. 'You see this?'

'See what?' I asked.

>   *Pointing at the script.*

'This.'

'Um. Yeah. I see it. I see it.'

'You do?' 'Yeah, yeah, I do. I see it.' 'Good. Great. Cause that. That right there. That page. I can do that with a look.'

'With a look. With a look. I can do that with a look.'

So, you know, I looked down at the page. At the words. The words written there. And I was like, "Great, man. Awesome." And he smiled and patted me on the back and walked away.

It's funny, cause you always hear 'the look' story. 'I can do it with a look.' For a monologue. I mean, it's Hollywood, it ain't New York, this is how it goes in Hollywood, if a dude says he's gonna do it with a look, then the dude's probably gonna do it with a look. And he'll probably nail it. Or that's how the story goes. The story usually goes, the writer's bullshit, how dare you talk about my words that

3

way, my words that I've written on the page for you to read, but then he gets over it, or you get over it, cause you're the writer, you take your bitter medicine, cause you're in Hollywood, and that's what writers in Hollywood do, they take their bitter medicine, and then you stand there on the set, and you watch, you watch as he gives the cameras 'the look', instead of the words, instead of the words you've written, and as the cameras roll, and you, the writer, and everyone else, sees 'the look', you're overcome with awe. Cause 'the look?' The look is fucking awesome. The look is fucking awesome. And then someone yells 'cut', and the director's talking to the AD or the DOP or someone more important than you, and the actor's getting a drink from his assistant, and you realize, goddamn it man, all you've written is a bunch of words, and that motherfucker, that motherfucker out there, standing around with people staring at him and wanting to touch him, that motherfucker, just said exactly what you wanted to say without saying a damn word. And you, the writer, is so overcome with emotion, beautiful yet confused emotion, that you can't speak. And the actor, as he leaves the set, later on that day, he maybe makes the slightest little bit of eye contact with you. And his eyes, man, his eyes, they tell you: "I fucking you told you so."

Or that's how the story goes. That's how I always heard it. Back in New York. Or when I moved out here. Fresh from the world of intellectual satisfaction and cold ocean air, fresh from the world of literary magazines and art museum cocktail events. Driving down the highway with my agent. Standing under some palm trees on Sunset Boulevard, feeling like a fucking tourist. At my first party in L.A. That's where, that's where, you hear it. Around. You always hear it. It's like an urban legend. 'The Look.' Come on. That shit doesn't happen, does it?

But it does, man. Three words. Like I told you. Three words. 'You see this?' 'Yeah, I see it.' 'This?' 'Yeah' 'I can do that with a look.' Ha, it was like finding the gold at the end of the rainbow. Like, wow, do I win I prize or something? Cause that just fucking happened.

But it's true what they say. Anyone who has the balls to say it, can probably pull it off. And I ain't gonna lie man... I didn't cry or anything, but when I saw it, when I saw 'the look', I was like, 'alright man, you did it. You did it.' Cause it was done well. It was done well.

I think you gotta trust. You just gotta trust each other. You know? When you're working creatively with others. You just gotta trust one another. Because we're all creative in this business, in one way or the other. But we're all different, too. So we just gotta trust each other.

Words, man. Words on paper. That's all they are. Words. I met with a producer last week. You know him, I'm not gonna say his name though. He was like, 'Why the fuck are you so wordy? Who are you, M. Night Shamaylan? What are you, trying to win a Golden Bear or something?'

'Fuck it,' he goes. 'It's good, just get rid of some of the words. Seriously. It ain't rocket science, and the people who are watching this shit, they ain't rocket scientists. Rocket scientists are too fucking smart to waste their money at the movies.'

We went out for lunch after. Got a beet salad at some new spot. They sprinkled paprika all over it. It was fucking amazing.

I don't know. Sometimes I think, 'maybe I'll go back.' To where I was before. But I don't know. It's only words. It's not life. It's only words.

Three words.

'You see this?'

WOUNDED

By Patrick Gabridge

MATTHEW: The thing is that I should be over it by now. And the fact that I'm not, the fact that I think about her a lot, often, frequently, not every day, but at least once a week. The fact that she's still with me... it worries me. How long does it take to forget? Maybe that's not the right thing to wish for. I don't remember exactly what she looks like, but I still remember how it felt to look at her. To whisper her name. To think, this will be my daughter. I've never seen such a small human being before. Fresh. For me, this was as close as I was ever going to get to a truly newborn baby. Not an hour old. Sitting there, under the heat lamp, looking cold and naked. Subject to the indignities of being helpless and voiceless. The nurse pricks her heel to test her blood, and she isn't gentle. Babies are tougher than they look, she reminds me. She has experienced hands--she's done this hundreds of times before. So I try to relax.

But how can you be relaxed when you're about to meet someone for the first time that you know is going to be part of your life forever. Hi, I'm going to be your Dad. You're going to be my daughter. This woman beside me is going to be your mother. Mom and Dad. That will be us.

And I know that there's a young woman about a hundred steps away, out the door, turn left, go to the end of the hall, take another left, and there she is. She's sleeping. She's alone, except for the social worker. And I'm thinking about her, somewhere deep in the back of my brain. But you are at the front of my attention.

They let me feed you. You weigh nothing. I'm used to the weight of our five-year-old, and I've forgotten how small babies are. Nothing. I'm the first one to ever feed you. I'm the one keeping you going on the continuum of life.

Love at first sight. I didn't really believe in it. That's not how it worked for my wife and me. Not even with my first daughter,

6

almost at first sight, but I was deathly afraid then. Now I'm relaxed, I'm not afraid of you. I know how to hold a bottle, I know how to nestle you in my arms.

Pictures are taken of us. Dad and soon-to-be daughter. I'd already made the leap. A name. An imagined future. We called our five-year-old--you have a new sister. She's beautiful. We'll be home with her in just a few days.

I wrapped you up and gave you back to the nurse. Back to the warm light. Until tomorrow. Until tomorrow.

And tomorrow comes and we visit, and you're in the arms of your birthmother. This is the time to spend for goodbyes. The impossible goodbye. I remember how you felt in my arms and I want to hold you again, but I'm willing to wait. In two days, I will have my fill of baby in my arms. We are silent and respectful--we do not ask, and we are not offered, the chance to hold you.

Another sleepless night, another anxious morning. And the social worker walks up to us in the hall, "I'm so sorry," she says. Like we should have already heard. Like we should have guessed. Like we should have already said goodbye.

But I didn't. I was suddenly reduced from potential adoptive father, to a stranger trying to comfort his wife. I only ever said, hello, welcome, this is us, this will be your name. Hello. But no goodbye. Just an explanation to your would-be sister. Just folding up the "Welcome" sign that she and the neighbors had so carefully decorated.

I should have shaken it by now. I have your replacement. I got a child. I can only think it's because I haven't had enough true grief in my life. As soon as a deeper tragedy strikes, when my parents or sister or children or wife finally die, you, my ur-daughter, will vanish, relegated to becoming the most imperceptible psychic scar.

But maybe it never heals. That's what's so frustrating. Because I know you changed me. Losing you changed me. And I don't want this transformation.

7

A SOLITARY VOICE

There are some substances that remain perfectly elastic and resilient, until one slight chemical change renders them tough and unyielding. I'm not the same man I used to be. I don't laugh as easily, smile as quickly. Do we have some limited number of internal receptors for joy? And if enough of them are damaged, do we transform into bitter, sour old men? I see myself on the cusp of losing touch with the brightness in my life. All has become dull and gray. And I don't know how to bring myself back to the man I was. And I'm scared to death I never will.

THE TUNNEL

By Greg Parker

BORDEN: When I first heard about cancer, I laughed. Heartily. It wasn't a product of shock or a way to cope; it was more a reaction to karma. It had finally come back to bite me. Moreso, it was karmic humor, I guess. I was always one of those people that was vulgar; foul-mouthed and spontaneous. I was that kid in class that always pressed the teacher who said, "One more word and we're going to be silent for the rest of class." As I grew up, I was the one that would tease girls too hard. I was trying to flirt, and instead, I was a virgin until I was 22. As an adult, I'd always tell friends, "Fuck off" or "Fuck yourself", or "Die in a hole". That was an especially good one. My favorite, however, was "Die in a fire". Just, rolls off the tongue. I said it to my friend Scott one time. Next day, he died in a house fire. He fell asleep with a cigarette in his hand. Poof. Gone. Two years later, told my friend Vinnie to die in a hole. Died four months later in a tunnel collapse while inspecting a mining operation in Wyoming. Last year, told my fiancée's brother to go fuck himself to death... I guess I was feeling especially good that day... And, you guessed: Died from an autoerotic asphyxiation fix gone wrong. I'm dead serious. Seriously. I'm like the "Good Luck Chuck" of death; I tell something to someone, it happens to them. So how does that bring me to my current predicament? Well, three weeks ago or so, someone at work asked me what my sign was. I said, "I'm a Cancer." Poof.

Of course, after the karmic irony passed, I was pissed. And depressed. Pissed and depressed. A terrible combination, I found out later, after a bottle of Jack and a sleeping pill. I also shaved my head preemptively. Bought a hospital gown, too. Has Elvis faces and toilets patterned on it. Hospital gowns are boring. Mine is amazing....Cancer makes you do some weird shit.

Naturally, I started to also think about death. A lot. Like. Every day. Especially on the shitter. "Is this gonna be my last one? Should I take my time? Enjoy it?" Stressful. The doctors are hopeful that I'll be fine, but how can they be sure? And even then, how can one *not* become obsessed with their own mortality? It was recommended that I attend a cancer support group. I went, mainly driven by that last question: How are these people dealing with that ever-persistent question: What happens when I die? Or even, "Have I done *anything* with my life?" Ultimately, I met a variety of people in various stages of denial, grief, and acceptance. And they all had a story. There was a priest who believed his prostate cancer was a challenge from God. There was a butcher who tried to kill himself when he was diagnosed with lymphoma. There was a small, round woman with no shoes who had just lost a brother to lung cancer. The last to speak was a tall, gaunt man with sad eyes and a cane. He struggled to stand, but when he spoke, his voice was loud and commanding.

"You all know me. And for those of you who don't, know that you're being graced with a presence that's two months past its expiration date. Since my diagnosis, I've done a lot of searching. My cancer is my own fault, a product of years of smoking. I accept that. However, as an agnostic, I've always been curious about what happens after. So, I was thinking a lot about it, and I think there's some logic to it. Death. Well, not death as a concept but, at least, the whole "white light at the end of the tunnel" thing.

Well, it makes sense if you believe in reincarnation. Which I don't. I think. I dunno. But. You see, when you die, that light at the end there? That, that *tunnel*, it's…. It's your next life, you know? It's the womb. It's… it's the transference of the soul. But along the way, you start to get stripped of your memories. You're fully aware of what is happening, of the years you're leaving behind; the loved ones you'll never see again, the loves you'll never get to love again, the children you'll never be able to kiss again, the trips not taken, the choices not made, and all of this overwhelms you. You cry out in grief and despair. You look backwards at the life you leave and you moan and wail and kick and scream. For a brief moment, you're suspended in between… there are *two* tunnels. One forward and one back. I've always thought that those who have a near death experience only got this far in the journey before being sucked back. But for others... you're there... in the middle... for a brief moment... suspended. Drawn out. Stretched between past and future... And then, just like that, you're wiped. You're wiped clean, and all that's left of your memory is the wail that expelled you from one life and entered you into another. The wail of a newborn child. And that's the cycle, isn't it? And... and that's some peace. I think"

He sat back down and, for a moment, no one said a word. Then the meeting moved on to the next person. I stared at the man, clearly on his last legs, and saw him look tiredly at his hands. The woman next to me whispered that this was the first time he had said anything in a meeting in over six months. I wondered how long he had been thinking about that. The end, I mean. *Pause.* It was right then and there that I decided that I couldn't.... I couldn't end up like that: Dwelling on the end to the point where I rationalized something that made sense and gave me comfort. I... needed comfort from the present, from the here and now. In a way, I guess, what he said saved me from all the thinking and wondering. Gave me comfort. But he was so wrapped up in the future, I imagined he had no desires for the present; merely to live and exist until it was time to go. I couldn't allow that. So... I invited him over. For dinner. His name was Steven. He loved books... and amusement parks... and... in the end... I... think he was happy.

A BOY LIKE ME

By Ellen Davis Sullivan

JOEY – Male, 14-16 years old, Black

JOEY: It's what our mom didn't do. She promised me she'd keep her damn job. No matter what happens, Joe, she says. Don't you worry. Even when all this Wall Street stuff starts and her company's all over the news. Yeah, you think I don't know what happens out in the world? Just cause you only use your phone to post selfies and text your girls doesn't mean I'm not watching how it's going down over there where our momma works. I gotta know. A boy like me's gotta know these things.

And every night when she comes home she says the same thing. She says, don't worry, Joe. Don't worry. Just keep studying. But I can't do that with what I'm seeing every day. The Dow's shedding points like dead umbrellas dumped in gutters. Whole banks gone. Did you know a whole bank can disappear? Not like 9/11, not windows shattering, glass flying, just like, bad numbers and more bad numbers then people go to take their money out and, poof, the whole thing's vanished. No money, no jobs, nothing.

Even when that's in the news day after day, our mom comes home every night and says, "Don't you worry, Joe. I'm safe. I won't lose my job." And you're not listening. You're just sitting there cross-legged, thumbs working like mad, eyes on your screen. Know why? Cause even if she loses her damn job, nothing's gonna change for you. But me, I'm different. I'm just one worn out pair of sneakers away from being somebody completely different. Just another guy in a hoodie.

You don't get how it is for me. No one looks at you and Mom together and wonders how you came out that shade. Nothing can happen to you. She can't afford tuition for private school? You'll do all right at Beacon High. Get your As, find some new girls to hang with. Not me. I lose Dalton; I'm dead. My only chance for college is if I graduate from a place no one expects a kid like me to get

12

through. My head needs that prep school halo hanging around it or I'm just another basketball wannabe, hoping to stick it out in college long enough to make the pros.

Don't make that face, that face that says I'm just like you. I ain't never been just like you no matter how much our momma loves me. You don't have to believe me, but I know how I get looked at in stores, on the subway, old white ladies flinching as I pass 'em on the sidewalk. Old men in the park tugging on their dog's leash, like what, I'm gonna grab some geezer's fur ball and run off with it? Don't look at me with your eyes half-closed like I'll be fine. I won't be fine. I know what this means. Mom lost her job and I'm doomed.

I'LL TELL YOU A STORY

By Amy Oestreicher

AMY: I don't have a story you hear every day. For a long time, it was a story I couldn't understand, like the sick plot of a psychological thriller. My life was out of control. I called a therapist. She listened to my flustered ramblings, then calmly replied, "You have to tell your story".

Tell my story?

"Yes, you have to say in words what happened to you."

I hung up and never talked to her again. She was oversimplifying things. I'm used to "thinking" myself out. I didn't know why I actually had to verbalize it. What could words do?

I spent a few months pretending everything was okay, but it wasn't. Then I thought, what the heck, I'll say it. I tried, but I couldn't speak.

At that moment, I knew the therapist was right. Until I could use the power of words to express what happened to me, I would not heal.

It took years before I could even articulate an idea of the turmoil that was rattling around inside of me. The confusion, the pain, the anger – the losses. In all kinds of journals, you know, the kind you see at Hallmark with the pretty covers and the inspirational quotes, like a compulsion – believing there would come a time when words would flow through me and guide me back to my _self._

Comes to desk, start to open journal, sits down.

And one day, I took one of those journals. I opened it. And I began to write.

Starts writing.

April 10th, Four-

Looks at watch, slams journal shut.

Oh, my mom is gonna pick me up for sound of music rehearsal, so I have like an hour to talk to you guys. Then I have dance class, then my friends want to get together – and my mom is driving me crazy about cleaning my room –I'm 13!! She's giving me a hard time about auditioning for the next show while I'm still rehearsing for this one - I'm so busy – and I love it!

God, I just love theatre so much. When I was a kid, I'd talk my dad into video-taping me for hours making these hammy home movies, and then I would force my brothers to be in them – they hated when I put makeup on them.

Oh, and I was at my friend's house the other day and she told me what an agent was.

I gotta get me one of those. How else am I going to make it out of Fairfield?

Comes back to journal.

April 10th. Four

Looks at watch.

Thirty-Two P.M.

Writing.

My parents are finally letting me audition in New York! I even convinced them last week to let me go into New York on a school day for a Broadway open call!

Okay, so I told them it was after school.

Okay, so I got typed out right away, which was a little discouraging.

Okay, so it was really discouraging.

But my mom totally blew that out of proportion and now she's telling me

Mimicking voice.

15

"how ridiculous it is to get yourself so excited and set yourself up for disappointment!" – but I don't mind the disappointment if I'm doing what I love to do! I see all the shows, I know all the composers, I've memorized all the lyrics to all my favorite musicals – I even tracked down vintage records of Les Miz in seven different languages! Hebrew, Korean, Spanish, Portugese... oh yeah, I had no idea they did Les Miz in Singapore, but thank God for E-bay! I was so excited that I took a picture of my computer screen, printed it and taped it into my scrapbook – just to prove it! My mom wants me to have a "normal" childhood - she's ready to pull the plug. You know what's normal? Messing up! So what if I got typed out on my first big audition? It gives my story some drama! Besides, theatre is just... something I have to do.

Flips to the next page and begins to write, somewhat quieter.

April...Oh I don't know. Things are good – I've been doing a lot of auditioning, I'm even performing! And, now that I have an agent, I'm taking the train in to the city for auditions – by myself...'cause I'm a woman now!

It's great – I'm really getting to know the showbiz crowd and feel like I have mentors in the crazy business – people I really trust. I think...

Quickly closes her journal and walks in the other direction towards a stack of three books on a desk.

I had some time to kill before an audition last week so I went to the bookstore . And I was browsing the Healing & Spirituality section – I needed some inspiring poetry to pep me up because I don't know, I've been feeling really drained – maybe that's just what this business does to you –

Picks up each book unenthusiastically.

"You Can Heal Your Life."

Drops book.

"The Artist's Way."

16

Drops book.

"The Courage to Heal."

Picks it up and looks closer at caption on cover.

"For survivors of sexual abuse."

Laughs, puts the book back, and takes a small step away. She suddenly pivots back, picks up the book, and starts to slowly flip through pages. She sits down, slowly, glued to the pages.

"Sexual Abuse."

Those are words that belong with plane crashes and gang rapes and armed robberies and dateline specials. In Fairfield, Connecticut, there's stress for final exams, or a fight with my drama-queen friends.

She looks around nervously, then continues to read.

"Check all that apply:

I feel dirty, like there's something wrong with me

Sometimes I think I'm crazy

I feel ashamed

I'm different from other people

If people really knew me, they'd leave

I have a hard time taking care of myself

I don't deserve to be happy

I'm a failure

I can't cry anymore

I feel as if my body is separate from the rest of me

I feel numb."

She stares at page in disbelief.

That's...my story. *Numb.* That was the word. The soft b felt tingly on my lips as I swallowed up that word in terrifying secrecy. Numb. That is how I felt. Like my body was physically going through the motions of everyday life, but the me I knew my entire life was not a part of it. It was as though I determined to remain in denial.

When I turned 17, a mentor who I had known for several years transformed into a complete stranger. One night I had come to his studio for a voice lesson. I went into total shock and coped by leaving my body and staying numb when he started to molest me. By the end of the night, I couldn't remember a thing that had happened. When I woke up, my voice teacher did not go back to who I thought he was. I stayed numb. For Months.

And months. Suddenly, all I could feel were my feet pacing back and forth over the endless passing of days.

Out of control. Until I could speak it. And... the therapist was right.

And then I was in a Barnes and Noble somehow holding an impossible book. Courage. Heal.

Nervousness rushed over my body, like I'd just been caught shoplifting. The warmth that filled my cheeks was a peculiar heat I hadn't felt since I had last laughed, or smiled. Words had the power to pierce through my skin with more potency than my fingernails, now rattling with uncontrollable energy.

So that's my story. And...

Realizing.

I've never actually told anyone before.

Holding journal in one hand.

Just this book.

Holding "Courage to Heal" in her other hand.

Only 'cause this book told me. So I guess I'm healing through stories – literally. 'Cause two stories talked to each other.

Holds the two books side by side

Sometimes you need other people's words until you can fill in your own.

Of course, some people like to fill in their own words for me. What happened that night. What I could've done. Should've done. Didn't do. what I did. Why I don't talk about it... I don't think of it as a secret anymore. I know it in my heart, and it's my truth. Just because I haven't shared his name, or have confronted him directly doesn't mean the universe can't hear my secret.

But I wanted to tell you too. I wanted to tell you, because finding that book, The Courage to Heal, a decade ago, I found words. That's all they were. It only became a story once I read them, and wrote out my own. I realized the value of my story once I was able to read it, and ultimately write it for myself. Ironic, that my mentor was a voice coach, a sociopath who so needed my silence.

But finding that book, I found music — more than words. A connection to the world. Everything was possible. I had a story to tell. And with a story, anything could happen. Even the good things...

She opens her journal, sits down and begins to write.

NECKTIE

By John Minigan

In a dark closet, an overhead light turns on, illuminating
EDDIE, a yellow patterned necktie, isolated center.

EDDIE: (angry) Oh, it is about time, I think. Can I just ask you, where you been? How long you think a necktie can just hang here in this dark, stuffy— With nobody turning on the light—

Oh, no. Ellen? What are you doing here? This is Patrick's closet. I've been waiting for Patrick for a week. I figured, fine, casual Friday, then the weekend, no big deal, but where has he been? Ellen? I know you can hear me, Ellen. What are you—? Where are you taking that shirt? I for one do not believe the idle threats:

He mocks her.

"If you do not stop seeing her, I'm changing all the locks and giving all your clothes to Goodwill!" Oh, really? Just the one shirt? I understand passive-aggressive, Ellen, but that is a Brooks Brothers shirt. Nobody who shops at Goodwill deserves Brooks Brothers. Ellen? Okay, let's be reasonable. I understand maybe you're mad. I understand he cheated on you with Christine, but that is no reason to take his best shirt and— That is a Ferragamo belt, Ellen! Do not— Oh, my God, the woman is impossible. No wonder he slept around. No, not the Testoni lace-ups! Put them down. Put them down before I get angry! Is it any wonder the man has been behaving the way he has? Of course he hasn't wanted to take you out. Of course he's been drinking more. What are you—? No. No! You are not giving away the Armani. Do you have any idea what happens at Goodwill? Do not touch the suit. I know for a fact that— Ellen, he said that's the last suit he's ever going to wear, so do not give it away. He told you he wants to be buried in that suit, so...

He wants...

Oh, my God. He wants to be buried in that—

Oh. My. God.

20

Ellen, pick me? Please. I know Christine bought me, but I was his favorite. I really was, so, just, please, pick me? Please? Let him wear, just one last time.

His eyes brighten.

Oh. Oh. Oh, thank you, Ellen!

He reaches forward.

THE NEW COLOSSUS

By Eugenie Carabatsos

NEW COLOSSUS enters, carrying his torch—a garbage can with flames.

NEW COLOSSUS:

Here at our sea-washed, sunset gates shall stand
A mighty woman with a torch, whose flame
Is the imprisoned lightning, and her name
Mother of Exiles. From her beacon-hand
Glows world-wide welcome; her mild eyes command
The air-bridged harbor that twin cities frame.

"Keep, ancient lands, your storied pomp!" cries she
With silent lips. "Give me your tired, your poor,
Your huddled masses yearning to breathe free,
The wretched refuse of your teeming shore.
Send these, the homeless, tempest-tost to me,
I lift my lamp beside the golden door!"

That's from a poem about me written by Emma Lazarus. It's called "The New Colossus," though you probably know me as Lady Liberty. Personally, I prefer the New Colossus, because, well, I'm not really,

Refers to man-parts.

ladylike. And colossus, well, colossus is one of those words that's just really... impressive. And the whole "new" part is great too because that means I'm young and relevant forever.

Except... lately, I haven't felt so... necessary. Not a lot of immigrants come by way of boat. I was closed for far too long for repairs. And damn this torch is like, really fucking heavy.

I want to feel connected to something again. The way I did back when Emma Lazarus wrote a poem about me. I had a purpose then. I was the watchman, the gatekeeper, the doorman to a world. Now I'm just... a symbol of the symbol that I used to be.

So I thought, hey, why don't I find my roots, you know? So I was like—okay, France! Because, after all, I was a gift from the French government and everything, but then I thought about it and realized—why would I want to go back to the country that gave me away? So yeah. I decided against France. Then I got to thinking—hey, if I'm the *New* Colossus, then who the hell is the *Old* Colossus?

Turns out, it's the Colossus of Rhodes. He's Greek. Ancient. His name is Helios. He's the personification of the sun. That's like. Wow. Right? I mean Liberty is cool and everything, but the Sun? I gotta meet this guy. He's sure to know everything about the world. He's sure to have the answers to all of the questions I've thought about for ages and ages. The only problem is... he was destroyed in an earthquake a long, long time ago.

I was inspired by him, some say.

HE sees the torch.

He had one just like this. And he held it up,

HE holds it up.

just like I do, to the sky, the sun.

HE looks at the sun.

They say when statues die we become the essence of the thing we are personifying. We are no longer trapped by our materials.

HE places the torch on the ground.

HE stares at it.

The Old Colossus is the sun, now.

HE climbs in.

Give me your tired, your poor, your huddled masses yearning to breathe free. The wretched refuse of your teeming shore. Send these, the homeless, tempest-tost to me. I lift my lamp beside the golden door.

HE's gone.

HE's free.

swooping for pearls

By James Celenza

Enter an elderly gent, sprightly but the years have taken what they will. His name is Chuck if you prefer.

Advances center stage. Halts, wanders somewhat aimlessly. Halts. Sees something on the ground, bends to examine it; deeply puzzled, tentative; picks it up; a small black notebook. He tucks it away.

He moves stage right. Then back. Stops just a stroke off center stage to face the audience. Peers out. Shrugs. Moves off as if to exit. Halts, moves back to off left center. As if someone had called out-'what did you just pick up?" He moves like one who has been forcibly moved by the police, by private security, by night hawks who prey on refugees the homeless and the lonely.

CHUCK: When I was politely informed that you were dead... they said it had been painless, they said. And that I need not come... It might prove... embarrassing, they said.

That was news I anticipated... Already recited Kaddish...

But, it was her granddaughter... Lilly, the skating ballerina with twin pigtails like silk woven ribbons had asked after me.

Only then did I learn, they had lied. That you suffered excruciating inexhaustible pain.... Had been besieged with tubes and probes and IVs which did nothing to staunch the inevitable.

Loud and accusatory.

Contrary to the directive you had left!

He shrugs as if that is that. Moves off, either stage left or right. Stops, reverses. Halts, as if he has lost his way. Shrugs as if there is no way to avoid the inevitable. Moves a few paces but starts to limp. Lowers himself slowly to the stage to face diagonally to the right side of audience. Removes his

24

shoes to massage his feet. One large toe extends from a hole in a sock.

Sing song with rhythm.

Somewhere her handprints...remain in concrete,

And somewhere her name remains in concrete...

It's always her face I'm looking for ...on every street...

Twists to face full audience.

Odd the lines you remember ....

And words. The words. Sometimes they support like bone; sometimes they will sever the carotid artery... Words.

Delivered as if lecturing a class of medical students. Perhaps he was once a professor of medicine?

There is a procedure during cardiac surgery whereby we must deliberately paralyze the heart ... *CARDIOPLEGIA...*

Rests his fingertips to the center of his breast.

Well, yes, 'times the bugger will go off line and off script. Maladies of the Heart... Overjoyed and over juiced as when the electric ping ping goes a'bonkers; either upstairs in the loft chambers or down in the basement chambers.

Times it beats remorsefully... as if trying to recover lost hopes and memories like boats against the current. Sometimes, of course, it is painfully disdainful of its owner. And then, sometimes it's the owner who is disdainful.

My old man refused to have his heart valves taken in for repair and recalibration. He wanted only to be reunited with his wife of forty-seven years. An outcome which occurred in his eight decade while saying his morning rosary in the chair by the window in a hot summer morning before the birds had awoke to pledge their fitful songs for the day.

I am of a mind to extend the definite description 'Cardioplegia' to other domains... Maybe to include it in manuals for raising pigeons on tenement roofs or chickens in the backyard? Or in an instructional foldout that explains how to rewire a VCR or how to play golf??? And, perhaps in a study guide on how to write plays?

Pause to ponder.

Ah shit. I am an old stupid fool... leave it be.

Wiggles his toes at the audience.... Arises. Gathers himself to make another push against the black heavy darkness.

As if to explain why he must now move on; and so hesitates.

Sometimes I venture down to the waterline and will find feathers and splintered bones scattered like the aftermath of a saber's slash.

Suddenly become aware of the boom boom of waves as they pound the beach: as if an echo from distant napalm- bombed lands. Soldiers and civilians stumbling headlong into the dark as their life contracts. And so.

And so to soothe my worried mind I recount the swirling contrapuntal of a Bach fugue. Daydream about ballerinas summoned and supported by elegiac winds stretching their nimble limbs waiting in line to perform the skating waltz.

He goes off left in his stockings. Stops... moves stage right... stops as if blocked by an invisible fence. His shoes are still on the stage.

I suspect the future may well resemble the unforgiving past. Skating ballerinas... Contrapuntals... Soldiers stumbling headlong into the dark.

Pauses, squats to pull his shoes on.

If only you could have been spared? With all the love I had, but it was never enough.

Pause to take a nose rag and blow his nose.

When first I saw you sitting across the classroom waiting for the lecture to begin.... It paralyzed my heart.

Chuckles softly. Wipes his shoes with the nose rag.

I have learned after all these heart-crushing decades is that the only thing that can fill you with more regret than death... *is love...*

Pauses as if...as if...

And so when tornado warnings are issued... I continue to travel through the bleak withering rain on our nation's highways... I do not seek shelter. I keep to the road.

Slight hesitation.

After all... What shelter can there possibly be?

Gathers himself as if to depart. Recalls he found a little black notebook. Extracts it from his jacket; examines it for any clue. Skims through methodically, page by page. He finds a page that captures his attention.

Reads.

Life contracts and death is expected, /As in season of autumn./

The soldier falls.

He does not become a three-days personage./Imposing his separation,

Calling for pomp./

Death is absolute and without memorial,/As in a season of autumn,/

When the wind stops,/When the wind stops and, over the heavens,/The clouds go, nevertheless,/In their direction. *

Closes notebook; tucks it away; prepares to leave.

Had I not a proper walking stick when I set off this very day?

Pauses, looks about full of puzzlement...

...Like an old shillelagh.

Scans the audience as if to plead....'have you seen it?'

A present from herself. 'Useful to ward off the ill winds and demons.' She wrote on the card.

Wistful.

'You old fool...'

Suddenly furious, he winds up as if he had his stout oak stick and strikes out against the darkness. It exhausts him and he barely retains his balance. Pauses to steady himself.

Did I leave it at my last stop? That warm, clean bright café by the abandoned streetcar line. And wasn't it myself to be enjoying a pot of tea at the tiny table by the window overlooking the gleaming bay below? Squawking seabirds skying and swooning to skim along the water's glittering surface swooping after the sun's glittering sparkles... as if they were pearls.

Moves off slowly. Glances about. Stops.

Squawks aloud.

CAW! CAW...

Smiles.

Exits.

O.S.

CAW!

Wallace Steven

RONNIE'S CHARGER

By Lawrence Kessenich

WAYNE: Looking at it, now, you'd never guess how sweet this car looked, sitting beside the garage on the bed of white gravel Ronnie and I put down for it. It was his first car, and he went all out. A neighbor who used to teach English told me about an essay called "The Kandy-Colored, Tangerine-Flaked, Streamlined Baby," and that's exactly what Ronnie's Charger was. He'd saved up for the down payment all through high school, and the day after he graduated, he bought it. He was enlisting in the Marines in a few months, and he wanted to enjoy every minute of the summer.

He did, too. He'd glide down Main Street with the windows wide open and the stereo cranked up, and the girls would all call out, "Hey, Ronnie! Nice car!" He could have had any one of them—he was a handsome boy—and I suspect he did have a few that summer. Most nights, he didn't come home until the wee hours of the morning. It was hard for his mother to let go, but she knew she had to. He was headed for Vietnam.

Men. What a crazy bunch of assholes we are. Always something to prove. I had to prove I was a man by going off to the Korean War. Ronnie had to prove he was a man by volunteering for Vietnam. And for what? To try to stop some other asshole men from kicking the shit out of their own countrymen. Craziness. Men can't *give* life, so they prove their importance by *ending* it. Shit. The sooner women take over this fucking world, the better, if you ask me.

I took the Charger out regularly, just like Ronnie asked me to. I'd cruise the main drag, like he used to do. I was a young forty, then, and the boy took after me, so I had girls calling out, "Hey, Ronnie," to me, too. I can't say I wasn't flattered—even tempted, a time or two, but I was good. Hell, Barbara would have shot my ass off with a 12-gauge if I'd messed around, so I guess I was more scared than good. It was nice to get the attention, though. It made me feel younger.

29

We didn't hear from Ronnie much. Hell, when you're that age, the last thing on your mind is your parents. He was out in the world for the first time. We'd hardly ever left the Midwest when he was growing up—couldn't afford it—so he was finding out that the world is a big place full of strange things. He loved Vietnamese food—just like I loved Korean food when I was in the service. Not a lot of either in Staghorn, Wisconsin, let me tell you. The few letters we did get were full of life. He didn't write about the heat or the leeches or the brutal firefights. He talked about the jungle flowers and the palm trees and the new buddies he was making. Maybe he was protecting us. Maybe he just didn't want to put that crap on paper—maybe it was his one chance to put a positive spin on it all.

That feeling younger driving Ronnie's Charger... Well, that all drained away the day Lieutenant Nietschke showed up at our door. I'll never forget his name. I remember looking at the tag on his uniform—white letters on a black background—and wondering if he was related to Ray Nietschke, the great center linebacker for the Packers. But once he told us that Ronnie was missing in action, all thoughts of football left my mind. I haven't watched a game since. Not one. Can't bring myself to do it. It was one thing Ronnie and I did together that never changed, even when he turned into a smart-ass teenager who didn't want to be seen with me. He'd still watch football on TV with me. We'd bitch at the refs together, leap off the couch and holler when our team scored. We had a good time.

Having been in Korea, I knew all too well that "missing in action" often meant blown to bits so small they couldn't be found, but I spared Barbara that information. She was so proud of how she was taking care of the Charger. She would go on about how happy Ronnie would be when he saw it. She kept up the weekly washing and waxing for a year, while I turned gray and fought with myself just to get up out of bed every morning. Barbara, on the other hand, would jump out of bed, peak behind the shade, see the Charger out there next to the garage, gleaming like the day it was made, and she was ready to take on the day.

That changed when we got the letter declaring Ronnie "presumed dead." Awful as it was, that letter helped me come to grips with reality. It was better for me to know that Ronnie would never come back than to hope against hope, day in and day out. But it took the life out of Barbara. She never touched that Charger again. As far as I could tell, she never even looked at it. She quit her job and took to her bed for three months. We could get along fine on what I made, so I didn't argue with her—not that she would have listened. It was as if she could hardly hear me anymore. I took her cold cereal or hot oatmeal for breakfast and soup or salad for supper. She wouldn't eat anything else. God knows if she even ate lunch when I was at work. She lost thirty pounds over those three months—and this was not a woman who had thirty pounds to give away.

At the end of the three months, she got up one day, put on her work clothes, and went downtown to get her job back at the insurance company. They were short of claims adjustors, so they were glad to have her back. She hasn't said Ronnie's name, since.

A couple months ago, a pair of raccoons climbed a discarded crate and got into the Charger's sprung trunk. They nested in a pile of rags Ronnie used to keep in there for when he worked on the car over at his friend Bob's house. A few weeks ago, those raccoons had babies. That half-open lid shelters them from the sun and rain. My neighbors are pissed off. They've wanted me to haul away this rusty hulk for years, but no one has had the balls to say it, considering who it used to belong to. They give me hell about the raccoons, though. They say I've got to get those animals out of there. But they don't understand. There's life in Ronnie's Charger again...and I just don't have the heart to end it.

THE DRIVING LESSON

By Shari D. Frost

(Inspired by true events)

At rise, a chair functions as the passenger seat of a car. SHARI, 50s, sits and fidgets, purse at her feet. She looks straight out the windshield.

SHARI: This is a terrible idea!

I'm sorry. This is not what you need. I'm making you nervous. I'm the last person who should teach anyone how to drive. I didn't even teach my kids how to drive. When's your road test agai?-- Um.

Person. Per-- Person crossing. In the crosswalk...

Beat, then with forced calm.

You see her. Of course you do. You see her. All good. It's all good. Don't listen to me. I'm sorry. Forget I'm here. Just... do your thing. Just... yeah...

Beat, then with forced positivity.

You're doing so great...! Great job! This is... this is fun... Why am I stressing? I don't need to stress. You're the one driving. In a foreign country. A long way from Iraq. Marblehead, Massachusetts is a very long way from Iraq. Why am I stressing? I'm just gonna sit here. Let you do your thing.

SHARI looks out the window, checks her make-up in the visor mirror, rummages through her purse, anything to pass the time, until...

Pointing.

Um. You might wanna-- Here. Turn here-- Quick! You have to get over. You're in the wrong lane! Turn left. Wait... or is it right? I forget. I don't know this road. I don't know. I don't--

Ugh... I'm making you nervous again. I'm sorry.

32

Checking out the street and surrounding.

Yeah, okay, we're good. This street's good.

I mean, I know what it's like. To be alone, in a strange land. When you're first married. I moved when I was first married. Except, well, okay I wasn't a refugee. And my husband came with. I didn't have to wonder if he'd ever be allowed to join me. And my whole family was right nearby. But still... I moved. Just like you. From New York. To a far away place...

New Jersey. It was hard. New Jersey. Starting over. Leaving the subway behind for a Subaru, while Siri was still the stuff of Star Trek, and GPS was, I don't know, a typo for UPS? Driving was disorienting. No one to lead the way. No one to tell me, should I keep going? Or maybe, turn back? Or left? Or--? It takes courage, right? Going out of your comfort zone. I at least had the luxury of comfort zones. My home wasn't a war zone. Not even a danger zone. I'd moan about 'no parking' zones. Yet now I'm walking around inside my own personal buffer zone?

SHARI returns to looking out the window. Long, uncomfortable silence. Until...

Pointing.

Um. Red. Well it's yellow but... you know... they turn red... quickly! I should have a brake pedal. Why don't I have a brake pedal?! That should totally be a safety feature. I'm gonna email Toyota. How could no one have thought of that? I mean do the math. You get like fifty air bags and only one freaking brake pedal?

This is so not what you need! Sorry.

Long beat, then trying to alert without alarming.

So this street is super narrow huh?

Kinda reminds me-- I mean it's totally different. But, I went to Havana a few years ago. The streets there, super narrow. Like Marblehead. In Havana Viejo. Old Havannah. Smells like Marblehead too. The Malecon? Salty and seaweedy and sandy.

33

Makes sense, it's the same water I think, courtesy of the Gulf Stream. We all have to share, right? It's just one globe. So, I'm in the backseat. Teal 1950s Chevy. A cab. And we're looking for my Grandpa's street. Where teen Grandpa lived. After and before. After Russia. And before America. We have his address. But the cabbie -- he's so determined -- but he can't find it. Keeps pulling over. Hopping out. Showing the address. Asking everybody, "Conoces esta calle? Do you know that street?"

I didn't tell you my family fled Russia, did I. As refugees. Waited in Cuba for five years. Didn't speak Spanish. At first. Weren't particularly wanted. Five years. Waiting to get into America. Only to be... All. Split. Up. Like your family. The cabbie was all like, "Que lastima?! What a pity we can't find it!" My quest was his new life's mission. His disappointment was visceral. I get it now. My story became a chapter in his story. From then on. Like your story is a chapter in mine. From now on. And they are crazy stories. I could be Cuban today. Or Israeli. You could be Swedish. Or Syrian. But instead, we're both American. At heart, anyway. Which maybe, matters the mos--

Stepping on non-existent brake.

STO-O-OP! THAT CAR'S STOPPING! It's... It's... Why don't I have a brake pedal?! I should totally have a brake pedal! How is it possible we can invent Bluetooth, and cars that park themselves, and no one ever thought about a passenger side brake package?! I'm gonna email Toyota. I am. I am! Because...

SHARI looks at the driver.

because I clearly have too much time. To worry incessantly about seriously stupid stuff. You're doing great. Just, just keep going.

Looking out the window.

Look at you, working two jobs. Getting home at midnight every night. Busting your butt. And still finding the time to learn to drive. Sort out your wife's documents. You're keeping the American Dream, or what's left of it, alive and well. You're so like my grandparents. Me? I was... born. Born in America. Born. And bred.

Under a lucky star. With a silver spoon...

Beat, then pointing.

My street. We're back. Back home. I hope you're starting to feel like Marblehead's home. At least your home away from home. While you build a home. Of your own. Let's stop in. Everyone will want to say 'hi!'

Beat, then with realization.

This was a good idea. Just what I needed.

ODYSSEUS RETURNS

By Donald Tongue

After ten years fighting in the Trojan Wars, followed by another ten years enduring an arduous odyssey, the heroic king, Odysseus, returns to Ithaca to discover a legion of suitors who have taken up residence in his palace: eating his stores of food and getting drunk on his wine, while they wait to see who Penelope will choose to marry. Odysseus decides to resolve the situation in a fashion befitting his status as a legendary Greek warrior - and a massacre of epic proportion ensues.

As Odysseus finishes his vengeful conquest, plunging his sword into the heart of the last breathing suitor, Penelope enters the hall.

At rise, a bloody and exhausted Odysseus stands in the center of the hall, firmly gripping the hilt of his soiled sword, while the tip of the blade rest on the floor. As he surveys the barbarous scene, he clings to a sense of self-righteous pride. He then turns and sees Penelope standing at the main entrance of the hall: statuesque, unable to move, her eyes frozen, staring at a husband who she can barely remember.

ODYSSEUS: (a hoarse whisper) Penelope... (slowly finding his voice)

To once again find myself staring into those pools of light that, for far too many years, I have only been able to imagine in my sweetest dreams... If I were to stretch my imagination to its outer most limits, it could never conjure the miraculous vision that now stands before me.

ODYSSEUS spreads his arms wide to welcome her embrace - PENELOPE does not move. He waits for a response, but none comes. His arms fall to his side.

Yes, your hesitation befits the moment. Now is clearly not the time for our long-awaited embrace. In truth, you are not to be here. Had you drunk of the intended potion you would have slept, and then awoke to find your long-endured nightmare vanquished. Always the clever girl. No doubt you puzzled out the plot - and your handmaiden now soundly sleeps in your place. Her snoring must surely be rattling the washbasin in our chambers.

Go, rouse your slumbering servant, make ready for our proper and glorious reunion. I will rid our banquet hall of these foul corpses, purge it of this deluge of blood and entrails, and then ready myself to join you.

> *PENELOPE does not heed his command, but remains stock-still.*

> *ODYSSEUS turns away and readies himself to clear the dead suitors from the hall, but soon realizes PENELOPE refuses to leave.*

Perhaps my prolonged absence has dulled my powers of discernment, for I find it difficult to read your thoughts and know your mind. In truth, I confess, I see myself as I would want you to see me, but that is not to be. Your eyes reveal a heart that has understandably grown accustomed to being alone. You look right through me, as though I were a ghost, an apparition of a man you once loved. And age can only magnify your suspicions - cause you to doubt me - yet, here I stand soaked in the blood of the many souls I have slain to make our world right and whole.

> *A long beat, testing.*

If you are not to leave, then join me. Let us work hand in hand to free ourselves of the stench of these shameless men. Then together we can bathe in the cleansing waters.

> *ODYSSEUS reaches out to PENELOPE to take her hand - she does not move. He becomes slightly annoyed.*

Surely you know that this is not a scene of my choosing. And you bear a share of the blame - yes. I am told you became quite skilled as a caretaker: increasing the flocks and the stores of treasure. With such wealth and no ruler to protect it - you welcomed this unwanted attention. I cannot fault them in their pursuits. Men are blind. The gods have placed a mask on the hearts of men - causing them to stumble about, not able to see - that they cannot see. Or perhaps they can see, but prefer to be blind, desire to be blind, blinded by lustful desires that drive men to pursue and pursue and pursue - and having reached the world's edge where all that awaits them is the abyss of eternal night, they pursue and pursue... and pursue.

Reflecting on his own acts of hubris.

yes, I admit - I too know this mask all too well. On one side, it can be a curse, but on the other - a blessing. Without it I would have become inert, frozen, unable to face my foes. Yes, the gods have given men the ability to be blind to what they face so that they can face it. Like these lifeless mortal vessels, I too have worn the mask for pursuits that caused me to lose all - my men, my ship, nearly my life - and perhaps my heart's greatest treasure... [you].

ODYSSEUS senses that PENELOPE's gaze looks past him. He turns, wondering if there is a suitor still alive. He quickly surveys the hall, then, once assured he has finished the job, turns back to PENELOPE.

If I did not know better, I might think you mourn the loss of one - or perhaps more - of these vultures. There were those who tested me - tried to make me doubt your faithfulness - telling me wild tales of the Ithacan Queen: how she seduced and pleasured a horde of suitors. I often played along, acting the role of the tortured jilted lover, which caused them to goad me all the more with stories of ever increasing offenses. Had they known their subject - like I - how she is ruled by modesty - they would not have spun such absurdities.

Be assured. Once I liberated the tongues of all who spoke ill of you, all such slanderous speech was forever silenced.

ODYSSEUS becomes increasingly annoyed by PENELOPE's inaction. A tinge of anger rises in his voice.

Am I to believe you have been turned to stone: unable to speak - or move - that you no longer possess a beating heart?

Or... or you have also heard tales: stories carried on the wind of a lost wandering king entangled in an odyssey - how he was ensnared by a goddess... He, a mere mortal - a man - powerless. She, a goddess. What could he do? He had no choice but to obey her wishes.

You must believe me when I tell you that, through all my foolhardy quests, my heart remained true, eventually guiding me to these shores that bear the name - home.

As ODYSSEUS reflects on his return, he is seized by a wave of righteous anger.

When once again I walked the road that led to our door, my heart sought a joyful homecoming - but no. I was greeted by men who made my heart ache with sorrow. Men so consumed by their base desires - they did not see me as I stood in their midst. Yet there I stood - witness to an array of false suitors who strained to erase any memory of me, longing to possess all that is rightfully mine to possess.

Begins as a menacing whisper, and crescendos into a thunderous roar.

Oh, my heart knew - my heart knew - the only way to bring an end to all we have suffered, to right all the wrongs we have endured, the only way to restore order to a universe ruled by fickle gods was to rise up and lay waste to the many many souls who would GLADLY BREAK OUR HEARTS!

PENELOPE remains motionless, a rock in the midst of the raging storm.

Why? Why does your gaze hold me at such a cruel distance? Why such a cold, chilling, silence? If only your lips would give breath to my name, surely the distance time has placed between us would fade like a mist. I pray you, look upon me, not with your eyes, but with your heart, the heart that once held me dear - hold me dear again, or else my heart's journey will have been in vain and would have met a better ending lying lifeless on a distant shore.

As before, they both stand motionless, staring into the eyes of the person they thought they might have lost forever.

ODYSSEUS, unable to bear it any longer, turns away in despair.

A single tear of defiance marks a path down PENELOPE's cheek.

I AM YOU

By Cynthia Faith Arsenault

Hey, stranger!!

I'm sorry. I don't know what else to call you.

That's how we roll - you and me.

We won't meet at a party, a PTA meeting, a fundraiser, or even the grocery store, so I'll never know your name.

And you don't want to know mine. So...

Works out well.

Am I right?

I'm right.

Though here's the thing:

We seem like strangers, but... we're not.

Actually...   I'm you.

I'm you — without:

The adoring parents;

Carters PJs — you know, the kind with the feet;

Teddy bear, named — what? Uh... "Bear;"

Family dinners;

Boo-boo kisses;

Trips to playgrounds, ice cream stands, apple-picking, or

Santa's Village.

I'm you — without:

Homework, clean clothes or teeth-brushing checks;

Nightly "tubbies" or bedtime stories.

I'm you — without

Anyone calling a teacher, caring about :

My grades,

My learning style,

My talents,

My frustrations,

My goals.

Yep, I'm you— without

The high school diploma— let alone the graduation gown, prom and after party;

Definitely without the college applications.

The Not You with the dependable car, fashionable suit, job interviews and cool apartment.

So — when you see me here on the street, I wonder what you really see.

Because when I look at you,

I see me —

And what could have been.

LISTEN UP!

By Andrea Fleck Clardy

Lights up on a middle-aged woman, any race or ethnicity, dressed neatly and casually. She enters stage right and moves to microphone center stage. She faces the audience.

The time is now, somewhere in the United States.

Good evening. Thank you for coming. I could start my comments with the usual list: "Superintendent Jenkins, Police Chief O'Malley, Members of the School Board," and so on. But I'm not going to do that. We know each other. Those of us who joined the District Task Force on Police Presence did so for one reason: we want the best for our students. Parents and community members here tonight came because we want to keep our children safe and help them learn. Am I right?

Exactly. So, here we are. We've all read the studies. We all know the tragic, heart-breaking stories. How many of you had a chance to look at the video I mentioned of an officer in South Carolina tipping a student over backwards in her chair, dragging her to the front of the room, and handcuffing her? Let's see. . . five, six. That's a little disappointing. I thought the confrontation in that video might provide an interesting contrast to the personal story I want to share with you this evening. Never mind.

As you know, I teach English here at the high school. Every November, I ask the students in my Honors Sophomore class to write about something familiar seen in a new way. Over the years, I've had kids write about how a lamp looked scary in the middle of the night; how their shy mom did the Heimlich maneuver on a stranger and saved his life; how a friendly neighbor revealed himself as a pervert. English assignments can create a safe space for kids to tell all kinds of secret stories.

A few years ago, a boy I'll call Jason wrote about a bunch of watercress in a little jar in the family's refrigerator. One night, the watercress went berserk and sent out huge branches that curled through the sealed door, under the linoleum, and across the kitchen walls, coiling out like great leafy snakes. By the time he got up in the morning, Jason wrote, the watercress had killed the cat. It lay on the counter with its yellow eyes open and its tongue sticking out.

At the bottom of the last page, I wrote: "A+. See me after class." Jason was a pale, heavy boy with neatly combed hair and horn-rimmed glasses. He lumbered up to my desk after class.

"Great story," I told him. "Where'd you get the idea?"

"Don't know." He stood there looking at his big shoes. Then he said,

"I got to thinking about things I'm not allowed to touch."

"Like what?"

"Like antique chairs in the living room. They're very delicate and expensive chairs. Or homemade chocolate truffles rolled in cocoa. Or, actually, watercress my mother uses in special sandwiches."

"Does your family have a cat?" I asked.

"No," he said. "My sister is allergic."

I've been teaching high school for twenty-five years, most of that time right here. Over the years, you learn a lot about which assignments work and which books the kids will like, and how to keep the classroom lively. You learn how to grade papers fairly and you learn how to watch for all kinds of trouble. Trouble is an integral part of the job.

The sophomores all read *Romeo and Juliet* in the spring. We talk about different reasons for keeping a friendship or a romance secret and why parents might tell them not to hang out with certain people. I ask them to think about how friendships that feel dangerous can still be appealing. Their assignment is to write a story about a secret friendship.

Jason wrote an introductory paragraph about how a close friend makes you feel more comfortable with yourself, more confident in your own potential. The right friend can earn you respect you might never get on your own. He went on to say that a friend who's forbidden is much more exciting. The most thrilling friendship of his life, Jason wrote, was with a Kimber Micro CDP 380, the most elegant handgun he'd ever seen. It evoked and I'm quoting him here, "a yearning to touch, a tingling sensation that swells into ebullience."

I copied the paper and sent it to our principal, Charlie McDonough. I asked him to join me in a conference with Jason and his parents. The following Wednesday, Jason sat in the back of my room after school, pretending to do math homework while he doodled tangled vines along the edges of his paper. Charlie wandered over from the front office, and eventually Jason's mother arrived. She was thin, with perfectly manicured deep magenta fingernails, and she was angry.

"Are you implying that there is something wrong with Jason?" she asked me. "He has a highly original mind and he is brilliant. Obviously. How many boys his age use a word like "ebullience" correctly? How many sophomores have his sense of irony?" She directed most of her remarks to Charlie, who nodded and murmured agreeably. But she leaned towards me, her eyes riveted, to say, "Whether we have handguns in our home is absolutely none of your business. The problem was the assignment itself," she said, "Enticing adolescents to focus on something forbidden has serious consequences. If you ask me, you're inviting trouble."

Then she stormed out and Jason plodded behind her, without looking at Charlie or at me.

When the door clicked shut behind them, Charlie said, "No wonder the kid has issues. Look. We've done due diligence. We brought our concern to the family's attention, and we had best leave it at that." He wasn't criticizing the assignment, he said. "But I can just imagine how a charge of enticement would play out. We certainly don't want to go looking for trouble." So that was that.

After *Romeo and Juliet*, I did a poetry unit with the Honors Sophomores. We were talking about the Emily Dickinson poem that begins, "Nature rarer uses yellow/ Than another hue." Jason raised his hand and when I called on him, he said,

"I brought my friend to school with me today. She's following the yellow trail. Anyone wearing yellow, no matter what shade."

I felt the adrenalin kick through my system even before I fully understood what he was saying. Time paused. Through the window behind his head, I watched a cardinal land on the windowsill. Its beak opened and closed, without a sound, and then it flew away.

"Jason," I said, "I want you to stay right where you are so we can continue this conversation. I want everyone else in the class—listen up!—to take your poetry book and leave the room quietly. This is a special assignment. Go directly to the library. Go there right now. You don't need a hall pass." I kept my eyes on Jason. "Jason," I said, "You and I will stay here."

When someone started to ask a question, I said, "Not one word. Leave. Close the door. Go to the library." As they trooped out, I leaned forward and said to Jason, "Just keep looking at me."

When they were gone, I walked around my desk and sat down on the chair nearest to him. "I'd like to meet your friend," I said.

"She's very shy."

"I'm not in a hurry. Tell her to come out slowly." He sat for a long time, still looking at me. I could smell the sweat from his armpits.

"She can't come out when I'm sitting down," he said. Then he stood up and I stood up, my heart thumping so loudly I wondered if he heard it. He reached into his right pants pocket and pulled out the gun.

"May I hold her?" I asked.

"You have to be very careful. She came to school seeking yellow. We're following the yellow trail."

"I'll be careful," I said. I held out my hand and waited for what seemed like a long time until the gun, small and heavy and oddly warm, settled on it. Then I thanked Jason, backed up until I bumped into my desk, made my way around it backwards, and put the gun in the top drawer. We walked down to the office together.

Jason didn't come back to high school. When he was released from the psych unit, he was sent to boarding school. Nothing was ever said publicly about what happened that day. The other kids in the class must have speculated but they never asked me. People come and go in their lives and the school year was nearly over.

If you were my students, this is the moment when I would say, "Listen up!" That's the preface for crucial information. In four out of five school shootings, at least one other person knew about the plan but failed to report it. I don't think armed guards will protect us. Listening, really listening, and building trust will protect us. For teachers, trust is what makes the difference between a job and a calling. It's what prompts kids to write to me sometimes from college or from Afghanistan or from rehab. I haven't yet heard from Jason. But he knows and I know that trust made the difference one spring day between a conversation and a tragedy.

Are there any questions?

THIN AIR

By Tom Coash

A woman wearing tights, a short black skirt, and an old sweatshirt stands atop a 2' x 2' platform. A 5/8th inch thick rope stretches straight out from the front of the platform into the darkness of the audience. The platform is isolated by spotlights.

BIRD: One foot in front of the other, one step at a time. That's how you do it. You're standing way up here on a two foot square platform. The wire snakes out in front of you, gently swaying, trembling with anticipation. The straight and narrow as Pop calls it. The hot smell of popcorn, horse-sweat, and the tang of the big cats. Center ring looks like a target for high divers. Spotlights tunnel up through the smoke, striking sparks off the glitter on your suit. There's the dizzying mad rush of circus music, animals, and the roar of the crowd echoing around the top of the tent. You take a deep breath, focus, and step out.

Karl Wallenda was probably the best... I mean of all time. The Flying Wallendas, funambulists of the first order. Tightrope walkers extraordinare. My heroes though were always the women. Miss Cooke, Lillian Leitzel, Josephine Berosini. And of course my favorite, Bird Millman from the '20s. You ever hear of her? She loved it you know. She'd run across that 36 foot wire like she was going to her wedding. My folks named me after her, Bird. Debuted when she was six years old. Soloed at twelve, then center ring for the Ringling Brothers. What I liked about Bird though was that she eventually flew the coop. Gave it up. Married her a Harvard graduate and quit the circus. Never went down once. Tightrope walkers don't use the word fall. It's 'come down' or 'go down'... or 'went down'. She never went down once and never went back. I admire that... knowing when to quit.

I've always heard voices in my head. All my life. Not like Martians or telepathy. I don't mean like that. I mean like... larger voices...

calling me. To larger things. Bigger things. Telling me to pursue my dreams. And I have. Sixty feet up on a five-eights inch steel wire. Without a net. Cause that's what life's all about it. Isn't it? Living without a net? "Look Ma, no hands." "Death defying."

On January 30, 1962 in front of 6,000 people at the Shrine Circus in Detroit, the Wallenda family came down off the wire. Fell as you would say. They were doing their famous seven person pyramid with sixteen year old Delilah Wallenda on top. An act they had been doing since 1947. Fifteen years. Dieter Schepp was the main under-stander. He was on the bottom of the pyramid with three others. They had two more on their shoulders and then little Delilah. All balanced on a five-eighth inch wire, less than two centimeters. Think about that. Think about the weight. All the support poles bent in towards the middle. Suddenly Dieter lost it. He was new to the act and lost his balance pole. He shouted..."Ich kann nicht mehr holten!"... "I can't hold on anymore."

I was pretty much born on the wire. Born to fame Pop says. Born to live in the eye of the needle. Mom says that I never kicked when she was in the middle of an act. Like I was helping her balance there on the wire. It is amazing when you think of living your life on a twisted steel wire no thicker than your little finger. Karl Wallenda said "that wire is your life." Literally. My Gran used to call it "walking in glory". Alejandro, my husband, once said "it was like stepping into fire." Referring I think to the spotlights but meaning something not unlike religion. Faith. Like those fire-walkers. A matter of belief. Belief that your skin won't burn, blister, and peel on the coals. Belief that you can do the impossible. Hubris. I looked hubris up in the Websters... exaggerated pride or self-confidence often resulting in divine retribution. I look things up so I'm sure, you know? I like things to be spelled out. Defined. Hubris. It's right next to hubcap.

You ever watch Wile E. Coyote and the Roadrunner? On Saturday mornings? My favorite was where the coyote stretched this rope across a huge canyon and then frayed it down to a thread in the middle. "Meep, meep" here comes the Roadrunner straight across, no problem. So the coyote gets mad and follows only to find the

Roadrunner poised there at the middle with a pair of big scissors. Snip. The rope slowly falls away from under the old coyote but not from under the Roadrunner. It's suspended in the air. You can see the realization on Wile E. Coyote's face that it's impossible and then...

She makes falling whistling sound.

...splat

I sometimes see the wire as the line between life and death. Before and after. Walking the edge. One step at a time. One foot in front of the other. Pretty much all wire-walkers understand in their subconscious that sooner or later they'll go down. Only in our hearts we don't believe it. We believe instead in grace... focus... will. Sometimes you start to slip up there and it seems like you hold yourself on the wire purely by the force of your will. The strength of your will. Like Gandhi or Martin Luther King. They changed the face of the world through the force of their wills. It's what kept them balanced on their high wires and what's kept me balanced on mine... at least that's what I always believed. 'Till now.

The first time I saw Alejandro Navarrra work the highwire I knew. His body straight and slender. Tempered, pliable steel forged in the fire of Mexican poverty. At the same time ethereal, elegant, old world. A proud man. He was the kind of man that would make the gods jealous. It was a beautiful thing to watch him. An intensity that made you forget there was a wire there at all. Just like he was walking in thin air. Or on water. We got married right there on the wire in front of a wildly cheering, Friday night Vegas crowd. He said he almost fell for me. When he put his hands on me and lifted me off the wire into his arms I felt my world shift and I suddenly had a new center of gravity. In him. It was no longer my force of will but his that kept me balanced. When he kissed me I felt like old Wile E. Coyote floating there, the Grand Canyon way below my feet. Holding me up with just his lips. Tightrope walkers tend to mate for life like cranes or eagles. There's a trust. A faith. Defying gravity together. Defying death. Maybe defying God. Hubris. Divine retribution.

When he went down... we didn't even have a year... when he went down... we were doing an outdoor show, see, and a gust of wind took him off. A small invisible push. The breath of a jealous god. Not two feet away from me. Like Michelangelo's picture..in the Sistine Chapel? God and Adam. I always thought those two hands were reaching towards each other. Now I know they were falling away. I was just there... left hanging in the void... and there was nothing I could do..can do..and now I have this loss, this emptiness. For the first time in my life I've become unbalanced. And I don't know what to do. Cause, see, you might have thought it was a flight of fancy when I compared what I do on the wire... my feelings, my beliefs..to Mahatma Gandhi. To some people that might seem frivolous. But it's everything to me. It's like an umbilical cord tying me to my family, my past, to life's meanings and mysteries. The wire has been my life. My path. When you're on the wire you know exactly where you are and where you're going... So why am I trembling? Talk to me Bird Millman. You knew when to quit. You knew when enough was enough. But god you must have missed it.

There's something I didn't tell you about when the Wallendas went down. Even though two of them were killed and Karl's son Mario was paralyzed for life, the rest of them were back on the wire in two days with a new act. Two days. Even little Delilah. It's a fact. It's legendary... I always wanted to be legendary... and this is the second day. This is my second day. I know it's just a matter of stopping this trembling... a matter of finding my own center of gravity again... finding faith and will... a simple matter of one foot in front of the other.

THE REVENGE BUREAU

By Andrea Aptecker

(a dark comedy)

A room in the Revenge Bureau. Mrs. Minsees, an officer of the bureau, loves her job. Her speech is crisp, she is professional, and her passion for her work is evident.

Minsees is an anagram: <u>Nemesis</u> - Goddess of Revenge/of Retribution and Indignation

MRS. MINSEES: Hello Linda, my name is Mrs. Minsees. Please sit down, won't you. I've looked over your statement in regards to your former boss, Brian Del Vecchio, whom you assert created a hostile work environment.

She glances at the statement.

He sexually harassed you—texted pictures of his genitals—on two occasions, he called you into his office, and removed his trousers— he groped you—and so forth. When you declined his advances, he terminated your contract. It says here you did report the abuse to human resources, but your words fell on deaf ears. They said Del Vecchio was too valuable an asset to the company, and you must suck it up, be a good soldier, etcetera. Well Linda, (peppy) he sounds like a first class dick, if I may be frank. You have a good case. If you're story checks out, you have various revenge options at your disposal. I have a list right here.

She looks at a list.

For example, we can hack his phone and computer, erase all his contacts, pictures, files. It will cause a disruption in his life. But I never like that one myself. It's too easy.

She looks at the list.

Oh, here's a good one. Feces in his bed, under the covers. We use fresh dog feces. You'd be surprised how effective it is!

She looks at the list.

Now this one is intriguing. The idea comes from a French movie, *La Moustache*. The main character shaves off his mustache he's had forever—years and years. *But*...no one notices. "Darling, you never had a mustache," his wife claims. He becomes paranoid. Has his treacherous wife set out to drive him mad? Let me tell you, nobody's more sadistic than the French, and that's a fact.

It's a delicate operation, but when done right, it's a work of art. He'll think he's gone bananas!

Does Del Vecchio have a mustache by chance?

Facial hair of any sort?

She awaits the answer.

Well, that won't do. Let me see...

She looks at the list.

Ah! We could cut off his toe. Now it may not sound like much, but hear me out. We send two field agents to his home, late at night, while he's sleeping. They tie him up, gag him, and cut off his toe. Easy peasy.

He'll need medical attention, and surgery, but his life will go back to normal, except whenever he's with a woman, he'll have to admit he only has nine toes.

She smiles.

He'll never get a date again.

Well, eventually he will. But it won't be with the cream of the crop. We women aren't superficial, but most of us like a man with ten toes. It's preferable.

Of course, someone who lost a toe through a calamity of no fault of their making, why that's understandable. People don't discriminate under those circumstances. But that wouldn't be the case here. And the good part is, word gets around.

She smiles brightly.

He'll be the douchebag with nine toes.

We prefer to cut off the big toe. It's emasculating.

I applaud you Linda, for wanting to get back a piece of yourself after what he did. You want to do something instead of sitting on your hands, like a nobody. *You* are not a nobody.

Forgive me if I sound uncouth, but pigs like him can't get away with it, I don't give a hoot or holler what anyone says. If men won't listen, we'll make them listen. And grovel. And crawl on their knees, begging for mercy. Just like women have been doing for centuries.

You worked hard, went to school, paid your dues, and in the blink of an eye, he destroyed all of it. He's a dream crusher. Well stand back Mister because you're about to get crushed. None of this *"turn the other cheek"* nonsense. Now that women are sticking together, we can bring down the pigs much quicker. I say, let them all fall, and if the companies who employ them don't do the right thing, the Revenge Bureau will.

You see, when a wrong has been committed, the universe is out of sync, and retribution must be taken. We're not supposed to live in an unfair world. People say, "Oh, well, life isn't fair, what can you do?" and to that I reply, POPPYCOCK. By righting the wrongs of a few bad apples, we can steer the universe back on its proper course of peace and justice.

Linda, my name is Mrs. Minsees, and I am an avenging agent of the Revenge Bureau. The enlightenment is upon us. I invite you to join the revolution, or be left behind. Each time a citizen stands up against injustice, she sends out a current into the universe that changes the course of history and breaks down the walls of oppression.

No man—or woman—is beyond the reach of justice. Have faith.

Now, how about a nice cup of tea?

SAMSON

By Don Cohen

WALLACE COOPER, eighty-five years old, sits in a wheelchair in the hallway of a nursing home. He wears a clean white shirt buttoned at the collar and dark trousers that are too large for him. He talks to an unseen visitor.

WALLACE: Fine, thank you. Fine. Holding my own. As the saying goes. No, I can't complain. (a brief silence)

Can't complain. First time this year they've got a window open. First spring day. Nice breeze.

(the following spoken, not sung)

The flowers that bloom in the spring. Tra la. Remember that one? Gilbert and Sullivan. *Mikado.* Have nothing to do with the case. It'll get cold again, I wouldn't be surprised. Nice for now. Spring breeze from somewhere. The South. Little flutter in the curtain there when a breeze blows, like someone's white dress.

Well. Open a window and half of them are chilled to the bone. Too hot yesterday, frozen today. Too hot, too cold, too dark, too bright, TV too loud, not loud enough. Enjoy fussing, if you ask me. Meat and drink to them. Make some noise, prove you're alive. Day or night there's no time you don't hear someone at it. A chorus of 'em, more often. Well, there's worse things. It's not my way, is all. Not my style. (brief pause) It's the nurses you feel sorry for. What they put up with. Thankless task. (brief pause)

Also the sins of their children—complaining about that. Supposed to be at their beck and call. As if they didn't have their own lives. As if there wasn't a world out there for them to enjoy. Never mind. If people want to complain, there's no stopping them. Life, liberty, and the pursuit of unhappiness. Hah! (brief pause)

I don't have much to tell you. No news is good news. Open a

window, it's an event. Red letter day. A while back we had something, a week or two back. Sound and fury that afternoon. One of 'em got away. Gladys. Escaped. Woman named Gladys, little stick of a thing picked herself up and walked out the door. They were short-handed, some of them sick, or other fish to fry. Not enough to go around. This Gladys made a break for it—absent without leave. Place in an uproar when they saw she was gone. They didn't tell you but you knew from the running up and down, doors banging. Came in here and looked under the bed! I said ... I told her, the nurse that's looking, "I haven't had a woman hiding under my bed for fifty years." Not that I did then either. They found her, still on the grounds, moving down the drive one slow step at a time: her getaway. Turned her around and back she came. "Where were you going, Gladys?" Nowhere, maybe. Away *from.* On the other hand, she's still talking about it: the ducks on the pond, cattails, daffodils. Sounds like a week in the country. And all the time they're looking for Gladys, the rest of 'em are squawking "Nurse! Nurse!" Calls of nature not answered. They're short-handed to begin with. Took more hours than you'd care to count to get this place half settled.

Nice little girl looked in on me eventually, at long last. Squeaky wheel gets the grease. It wasn't Elaine. A new one. Elaine went somewhere else: greener pastures. A sweet little girl, though. Doing her best. They appreciate if you see their side, you're not after them all the time, do this, do that. (brief pause)

I've still got my sight, still read. Glad of that. Clean clothes, a place to sleep. Know where my next meal's coming from. Food delivered, or they roll me to the dining room. Sometimes Mohammed goes to the mountain; sometimes the mountain comes here. It's not so bad. I read. Different things. I read the Bible some. Didn't used to. Not that I believe it now, not every word. Most I don't, but there's truth in those stories: food for thought. Great stories, some of them. Others I don't like. Abraham and Isaac? Asked to sacrifice his son? Hate that one. God says, "Go kill your son." Then changes his mind: just kidding, let him go. As if that makes it all right. Testing him. Blind obedience: keep your mouth shut and do what I say.

Brutal kind of a God. Bully. Tower of Babel's the same thing—knock down some else's blocks. Jealous.

You know the story of Samson? That's quite a story. Samson and Delilah. The Philistines. You know that one. I'll tell you something to make you laugh. Then I'll let you go. You know the story: Samson slaying Philistines by hundreds and thousands with the jawbone of an ass. Battles here and there. Delilah tricks him, learns his secret— he's strong if no one cuts his hair. She gives him a haircut when he's asleep and that's the end of all his great strength. Snip, snip and he's just like anybody else. You know the story. They capture him— and they blind him too. Still afraid of him. And tie him up, chain him. He's chained to the pillars of the Philistine's temple or whatever it is. So there he is, chained up and on display: thousands of Philistines in that temple mocking and celebrating. Their great enemy chained hand and foot, blind, weak as a kitten. Well, Samson asks God to grant him one last wish. He wants his strength back for just a single minute. That's his one and only request. God doesn't say a word but the answer is "yes." Samson feels his strength coming back, pouring into him like sap rising in a tree, like a flood, like a flame of fire. He pulls on the chains that bind him to those pillars, pulls and pulls and brings them down, pulls them to pieces, and the whole Philistine temple comes down, crushing those thousands of Philistines, killing every one of them. One minute before they're jeering and dancing, now they're smashed dead. Samson along with them, but he doesn't mind: out in a blaze of glory. I read that particular story one or two times a week. Funny part is—I said I'd make you laugh—the funny part is I'm sitting here, reading that Samson story, and I imagine it's me in that temple. I imagine I'm Samson myself. Isn't that a humorous thing? Samson! Hah! Samson. It's true, though. Because to tell you the truth every once in a while I get tired of this situation. A little tired of it, a little impatient, at times more than a little. It happens. Tired and you might say angry—I admit that too. Yes, angry. From time to time. So tired and angry sometimes I wish I was Samson chained to those pillars—yes—blind but strong again like I was, like he was and angry as him when he pulled those pillars down. In my mind I'm Samson—yes! hah! Samson!—bringing it all crashing down around me with the strength of my own two arms: all of this coming down, crashing, crushed to pieces once and for all! Everything! EVERYTHING!

Everything.

[DIS]CONNECTED

By K. M. Sorenson

Lights up on GIRL. If used, BOY is unobtrusive and separate from her, periodically texting and becoming more frustrated until he exits violently near the end of the play.

The sound of the arrival of a text message is heard - "Bing!". Optionally, the message "Wru?" is projected. GIRL resists at first, but then glances down at the phone to read the message.

GIRL: (brief pause, matter-of-factly) Did you know the average teenager sends and receives more than one hundred and twenty text messages a day[i]?

(astounded) That's over forty thousand messages a year! Maybe there are some outliers. Like we learned about in Statistics class. You know, the heavy users. That would be me.

"Bing!" is heard. Optionally, "Call me" appears.

(nervous) I should just turn it off, right? I mean, technology – who needs it? Yeah, sure. LOL. A teenager without a phone? That's like - like a man without a penis! Practically a pariah!

(matter-of-factly) "Pariah. An outcast. Originally referring to a member of the Parayar class in Indian society." I take Sociology right after Human Sexuality. (brief pause and small beat) I can't believe I said "penis." (brief pause and small beat)

So I can't just turn it off. I'd be – disconnected. I might miss something. Hey, I might. I do have a life. A boring life, but a life. School. Home. Sleep – when I can get any. You know – all the messages. Ten o' clock. One o' clock. Three o' clock in the morning. By that time, you figure, why bother?

"Bing!" is heard. Optionally, "Wru@!" appears.

I hate being here. Alone. Hated it was I was a kid - after school - by myself. Seriously, I always thought there was a zombie living in my closet, ready to jump out and - eat my brains! After my parents came home one day and found me hiding in a closet with a meat cleaver, they said "No more horror movies." Anyway, you'd think I'd be used to it. Being alone. But I'm not.

"Bing!" is heard. Optionally, "Uw tat guy? appears.

(beat, lighter tone) We met at the Junior dance. Two years ago last Saturday. He came with another girl, but she got totally wasted and spent the whole night puking in the bathroom. I don't know what I was thinking – I mean, he was *so* out of my league - but I asked him to dance. And he said yes! We spent the rest of the night together, and afterwards we made out and he put his hand up my bra.

(brief pause and small beat) Maybe I shouldn't tell you that.

"Bing!" is heard. Optionally, "Betta not b" appears.

My friends were all jealous and like "He is *so* cool!" But it's funny, because he didn't like them. He didn't like any of them. He said they weren't good enough for me. (serious) Only he was.

"Bing!" is heard. Optionally, "Call me" appears.

He wants me to answer. But - I'm not going to.

(defiantly) Not anymore. At first, I didn't mind. It was just a couple of messages a day. That's normal. Maybe even a little light. Then it was all day. Then all night. Oh, about nothing special. He just wants to know where I am. Who I'm with. What I'm doing.

That's all. Just everything.

(frustrated) At three o' clock in the morning what does he *think* I'm doing?!

"Bing!" is heard. Optionally, "URSLUT" appears.

I didn't tell my parents. It wasn't really that big a deal, you know? I figured he - liked me.

But then - at the Thanksgiving Day game - I was talking to my brother's friend, and he started this *huge* fight. About nothing! I was just talking! He punched a wall and hurt his hand and got suspended for a week. After that, I told him we should – maybe - take a break. You know, chill. And he was okay with it. That's what he said. "Okay." But it didn't stop. He kept calling and texting. Even cried one time. I was like OMG. I can't believe he's crying! He said he was sorry. He said he couldn't live without me and that he was really, *really* sorry. I think he was. But nothing changed. Actually, it did. It got worse.

"Bing!" is heard. Optionally, "Didn't mean that" appears. She almost gives in and responds, but she resists.

I know it's partly my fault. I shouldn't have left my phone out. I probably would have looked, too. One time I did. That's when I found out he was talking to his old girlfriend, Jenny. I totally freaked out. Then, *he* freaked out. Said *I* didn't trust *him*. Said I was a bitch. But *he* was the one calling *her*! And then he gets all super mad over one text. One stupid text about homework! I mean, really mad.

"Bing!" is heard. Optionally, "W fk ru??" appears.

(small beat) It wasn't always like this. Because he used to be a lot of fun. We'd go out with my friends. and we'd have fun. But I would always say something – or do something – and he would get upset and act up. Act out. Like a little kid. Or just be a total jerk. I think he did it on purpose. He didn't really like them anyway.

"Bing!" is heard. Optionally, "FUCK R U!" appears.

(small beat, gaining courage) So, I decided to do it. Really. In person, so he had to listen to me. So he couldn't ignore me. I told him to meet me at McDonalds. I figured I'd be safe there – you know, just so long as I didn't eat anything. But he didn't show up. I waited for two hours! I kept texting him, but he wouldn't answer. So, I went home. And he called me. Like nothing was wrong. Like he'd been watching me all along. Like he was right outside my house. I totally freaked. Told him I hated him and never wanted to see him again. I told him I didn't care if he hurt himself. "Go ahead," I said. "Do it – see if I care!"

"Bing!" is heard. Optionally, "U made me" appears. The text

messages come faster.

He'd done it before. I'd seen the scars. One time, he used a cigarette on his arm. Like a game. To see how long he could last.

"Bing!" is heard. Optionally, "Hurts like hell" appears.

I think he really needs help, but it's like I'm the only one who does! Everyone else thinks he's just intense – or moody – or something. But they don't really know him.

"Bing!" is heard. Optionally, "Want you" appears.

He's not a bad guy. He wouldn't do anything stupid. And he wouldn't really hurt anyone

– except maybe himself. But I don't think he would. I - hope. Because he does have it. The shotgun. His dad bought it for his birthday, do you believe it?

"Bing!" is heard. Optionally, "Wru!" appears.

I said to him "Do you know a gun in the home is more likely to be used in a murder or suicide than for self-defense?[ii]" I know. I did a project on it last year.

"Bing!" is heard. Optionally, "I got it" appears.

But he said he and his dad were just gonna use it to shoot pigeons. "They're dirty," he said. "They mess up the yard and stuff." (ironic) I sure hope I don't look like a pigeon.

"Bing!" is heard. Optionally, "Wit me" appears.

I'm not gonna look. (short pause) I am not looking! (increasingly anxious) I should just turn it off, right?

"Bing!" is heard. Optionally, "U no" appears.

(nervously) Technology – who needs it?

> *She tries to gain the courage to turn off the phone. Another message arrives ("Bing!) ("Do it" appears), startling her into action. She turns off the phone, treating it warily, as if she is defusing a bomb. If used, BOY exits from the view of the*

audience after the last message, optionally kicking over the stool or chair he was sitting in, which should startle the audience, but not her.

There. That wasn't so hard. Maybe – he'll stop now. I hope so. That would be the best. He's not a bad guy - just – troubled. Or - broken. Like a broken toy. Like a toy that used to be fun - but now only hurts you, gives you cuts and bruises. So, he just needs to find another girl. Someone who will make him happy. Everyone deserves to be happy. But it can't be me. I'm not that girl. Because I want to live. Like a normal person.

I just want to live my life!

A loud pounding on the door startles her. She turns abruptly and directs her gaze at the door, looking frightened.

LIGHTS FADE TO BLACK

[i] www.textrequest.com/blog/many-texts-people-send-per-day/

[ii] http://www.bradycampaign.org/facts/gunviolence/gunsinthehome/

APPENDIX A - PLAYWRIGHT BIOS

Andrea Aptecker's plays include *The Revenge Bureau:* Fem Noire Festival/Image Theater 2018, *Unrequited*: The North Shore Readers Theater 2018, You're *Killing Me Already!:* The Playwrights' Platform 45th Festival of New Plays and anthology 2017, *KKK Cookies:* Cambridge Center for Adult Education Evening of New Plays 2017, and *Goodnight Spouse*: CCAE Second Annual Festival of New Plays 2018. Andrea teaches public speaking in Cambridge, MA, and acts in local theatre. Recent roles include Lady Nijo/*Top Girls*, Dame Northumberland/*Henry the 4th*, Calonice/*Lysistrata*, and Suzanne/Countess/Admirer/*Picasso at the Lapin Agile*.

Cynthia Faith Arsenault, psychologist by day, writer by night, is a former director, whose playwriting group, co-founded and aptly named Group, encouraged her to take up the pen. Five years later, she is published this year in "Best of 5 Minute Plays for Teens," "Best 10 Minute Plays of 2017," and at Monologuebank.com. There have been over 70 productions of her short plays at Boston area venues— the Firehouse Ctr. and Boston Playwrights Theatre; Cohasset Drama; Hovey; Our Voices; Acme; Image; Company Theatre; Acton 3 and Actors Studio of Newburyport—as well as most other states, as well as in London, Canada and Australia. This particular epic monologue was written for a Chicago Homelessness project as part of a street performance initiative to raise awareness.

Eugenie Carabatsos's plays have won the Kennedy Center Harold and Mimi Steinberg National Student Playwriting Award, the Trustus Theatre Playwrights Contest, the Mountain Playhouse Comedy Writing Competition, the Venus Theatre Festival, and the University of Tulsa's WomenWorks Competition. They have been produced by Trustus Theatre, Stages Theatre, 2cents Theatre, iDiOM Theatre, and South Park Theatre, as well as in a number of festivals and development programs including the Great Plains Theater Conference. She graduated with her MFA in Dramatic Writing from Carnegie Mellon University in 2016, and received her BA from Wesleyan University in 2010.

James Celenza's plays have been performed at Perishable Theater for the Think Tank Festival, the New Ten Minute Plays Festival; other venues include Barplays Festival, Culture*Park Festival, Roots Cultural Center, What Cheer in the Park, Providence Fringe Festival, the Columbus Theater, Trinity Repertory Company Kickoff. A play *Analgesia* was published in Ars Medica, Univ of Toronto Press, spring 2012; and as chapbook by the PoetryLoft 2014. James co-produced the Station Nation: National Reflections on the Station Fire in collaboration with Soulographie and the Department of Theatre Arts and Performance Studies at Brown University (2013); and the Barplays Festival(2010-11) with the Words Progress Administration Collective. Member of the Dramatists Guild of America.

Andrea Fleck Clardy's short plays and monologues have been widely produced, from Alaska to Australia. Two of her short plays are included in *Best Ten-Minute Plays of 2016*, (Smith and Kraus). She received the Promising Playwright Award from Colonial Players in Annapolis MD this year and was part of the Last Frontier Conference on Playwriting in Valdez, Alaska. She has been a finalist for the Eugene O'Neill National Conference and the Princess Grace Award and twice for the Heideman Award. ACT IV, a community theater in Plainfield, NJ, created a full-length production of her short plays and monologues. HIDE AND SEEK, a children's play with music by Clark Gesner, premiered at the Hangar Theatre in Ithaca, NY. Educated at Swarthmore College and Harvard University, she worked in publishing for thirty years, at Crossing Press, ILR Press, and Cornell University Press. Her nontheatrical publications include a children's book, a series of calendars about remarkable American women, a collection of newspaper columns, two books about upstate New York, and a writer's guide to feminist publishing. A full list of productions is on her website at andreafleckclardy.com. She lives in Boston and is a proud member of the Dramatists Guild and the National Writers' Union.

Tom Coash is a New Haven, Ct. USA playwright, director, and professor. Prior to New Haven, he spent three years in Bermuda and four years teaching playwriting at The American University in Cairo, Egypt. Coash has won numerous playwriting awards including the American Theatre Critics Association's "M. Elizabeth Osborn Award", the Clauder Competition for New England Playwrights, an Edgerton Foundation National New Play Award, the Hammerstein Award, The Kennedy Center's Lorraine Hansberry Award, a Jerome Playwriting Fellowship, among others. His plays have been produced around the world including such theaters as: Portland Stage, Barrington Stage, the InterAct Theatre, Abingdon Theatre, Ensemble Studio Theatre, Bailiwick Theatre, West Coast Ensemble, and many more. His play CRY HAVOC was recently produced in the South African National Arts Festival where he was an artist-in-residence. His new award-winning play VEILS was one of six Finalists for the American Theatre Critics Association's ATCA/Steinberg Best New American Play Award. Coash teaches playwriting at the University of Southern Maine's Stonecoast MFA Writing Program.

Don Cohen's plays, *Length of Stay and Celestial Mechanics* have been performed as Munroe Saturday Nights staged readings. He has received a Massachusetts Artists Foundation playwriting fellowship. His stories have appeared in *The South Carolina Review*, *The Fiddlehead, Lifetimes,* and Jewish fiction.net. *Pilgrims of Mortality,* his collection of short stories, is available from Amazon.

Don is co-author, with Larry Prusak, of *In Good Company: How Social Capital Makes Organizations Work* and was writer-researcher for Robert Putnam and Lewis Feldstein's *Better Together: Restoring the American Community.* He was Editor-in-Chief of IBM's *Knowledge Directions* and Managing Editor of NASA's *ASK Magazine.*

Shari Frost's plays have been produced at the Boston Theater Marathon, the Warner International Playwrights' Festival, the New Works Festival, and Our Voices. *I Just Love That Keith Urban* is published in Smith & Kraus' *The Best Ten-Minute Plays 2017. Bang for the Buck*, a regional finalist for the Kennedy Center American College Theater Festival, is published in Smith & Kraus' *The Best Ten-Minute Plays 2015.* TWO LEFT(IST) FEET, ONE LAST DANCE was a national finalist for the Playwrights' Center's Core Apprentice Program. Shari is also the creator and producer of the TNT! - Totally New Theater - Playwrights' Collective and Festival. Shari's screenplays have advanced in the Academy Nicholl Fellowships, as well as the Final Draft Big Break and Austin Film Festival Screenwriting Competitions. She is currently a reader for the Austin Film Festival. Shari is a member of the adjunct faculty at Lesley University in Cambridge, MA, where she received her MFA in Creative Writing, with a concentration in Writing for Stage and Screen. For more, go to www.sharidfrost.com.

Erica Furgiuele is a Vermont-based singer, actor, and writer. She graduated from Middlebury College in 2015 with a degree in theatre and film. She divides her time between working at the Vermont Folklife Center, serving tea at Stone Leaf Teahouse, and teaching Shakespeare It's Elementary through the Courageous Stage Theatre Education program at Middlebury's Town Hall Theater. She loves baking pie and Italian opera. She is the 2013 recipient of the KCACTF Irene Ryan Classical Acting award. Off-Broadway: PTP's Pentecost, Marina.

Patrick Gabridge's full-length plays include *Blood on the Snow, Lab Rats, Distant Neighbors, Fire on Earth*, and *Blinders*, and have been staged by theatres across the country. He's been a Playwriting Fellow with the Huntington Theatre Company and has received fellowships from the Boston Foundation and the Massachusetts Cultural Council. Recent commissions include plays and musicals for the Brown Box Theatre Project, In Good Company, The Bostonian Society, and Central Square Theatre. His many published short plays have received more than 1,000 productions from theatres and schools around the world. He is the artist-in-residence at Mt. Auburn Cemetery for 2018-19, where he will develop new site-specific plays. He's also the author of three novels, *Steering to Freedom, Tornado Siren* and *Moving [a life in boxes]*. Patrick helped start Boston's Rhombus Playwright's group, the publication Market InSight... for Playwrights, and the on-line Playwrights' Submission Binge. He is the Dramatists Guild's Regional Rep for New England. He is the co-founder of the New England New Play Alliance and artistic director of the Plays in Place theatre company. In his spare time, he likes to farm and fix up old houses. www.gabridge.com

Greg Hovanesian is a playwright, screenwriter, actor, and producer in Boston, MA. His play *Water* won Best Play at the Playwrights' Platform 2016 Festival of New Plays (Boston Playwrights' Theatre). His full-length play *Thirsty* was produced by Ya Bird? Productions in 2016. His plays have been produced and developed by Boston Actors Theater, Boston Playwrights' Theatre, Hovey Players, Generic Theater, the Playwrights' Platform, Centastage, Image Theater, UAE Theatre Festival, and Ya Bird? Productions.

Greg is also an actor who was awarded Best Actor at the Playwrights' Platform 2016 Festival of New Plays. He is a member of the Dramatists Guild of America and serves on the board of the Playwrights' Platform, where he is Director of the Actors-In-Residence program.

Lawrence Kessenich is a playwright, poet, essayist, and former amateur actor. He has had sixteen 10-minute plays produced at festivals, one of which won the People's Choice Award in a national competition in Durango, Colorado. His full-length play *Anne Frank Lives!* was shortlisted for the Ashland New Play Festival. Kessenich studied theatre at the University of Wisconsin-Milwaukee and acted in amateur productions in Wisconsin and Massachusetts, including the roles of Tessman in *Hedda Gabler* and Chulkaturin in *The Journey of the Fifth Horse*. His poetry has been widely published, and in 2010 he won the Strokestown International Poetry Prize. He has also published a number of essays, reading "In My Father's Tears" on NPR's *This I Believe*, after it was published in an essay anthology. His first novel, *Cinnamon Girl*, was published in 2016. Kessenich lives in Watertown, Massachusetts.

John Minigan's plays have been produced throughout the US and Canada, Europe, Asia and Australia. He has developed new work with the Orlando Shakespeare Theater, New Repertory Theater, the New American Playwrights Project, and Actors' Repertory Theatre of Vermont. His work has been included in the *Best American Short Plays, Best Ten-Minute Short Plays,* and *New England New Plays* anthologies. He was a 2018 finalist for the O'Neill National Playwrights Conference, a 2015 semifinalist and a 2014 finalist for the Heideman Award at the Actors' Theatre of Louisville. He has had work selected for the Gary Garrison Festival and three times selected for the Samuel French Festival. He is a four-time winner of the Firehouse New Works Contest, a winner of the Nantucket Short Play Contest, the Rover Dramawerks Competition, the Longwood 0-60 Contest, New York's 8-Minute Madness Festival, the Nor'Eastern Playwriting Contest, Seoul Players Contest and the KNOCK International Short Play Competition. When not writing, John teaches theater, writing and Shakespeare. He is a member of the Dramatists Guild. Please visit johnminigan.com

Amy Oestreicher is a PTSD specialist, artist, author, writer for The Huffington Post, speaker for TEDx and RAINN, health advocate, award-winning actress, and playwright. She is a SheSource Expert, a "Top Mental Health" writer for Medium, and a regular lifestyle, wellness, and arts contributor for over 70 notable online and print publications, and her story has appeared on NBC's TODAY, CBS, Cosmopolitan, Seventeen Magazine, Washington Post, Good Housekeeping, MSNBC, among others.

As a playwright, Amy has received awards and accolades for engaging her audiences in dynamic conversation on trauma's effects on society, including Women Around Town's "Women to Celebrate" 2014, BroadwayWorld "Best Theatre Debut," and Bistro Awards "New York Top Pick." Amy has written, directed and starred in a one-woman musical about her life, Gutless & Grateful, touring over 200 venues, theatres, schools, festivals, conventions and organizations since it's 2012 New York debut, including Barrington Stage Co. and Feinstein's/54 Below.

To celebrate her own "beautiful detour", Amy created the #LoveMyDetour campaign, to help others cope in the face of unexpected events. Her passion for inclusion, equity and amplifying marginalized voices has earned her various honors, including a scholarship from the Association for Applied and Therapeutic Humor Professionals, the first annual SHERocks

Herstory National Performing Artist Honoree, a United Way Community Helper award, and a National Sexual Education Grant honor. More at www.amyoes.com

She was the 2016 keynote speaker for the Hawaii Pacific Rim International Conference on Diversity and Disability. and will be the featured keynote speaker at the 2018 International School of Social Work Conference in Ohio. www.amyoes.com

Greg Parker is a NH-based writer, director, and actor. In his free time, he is a social studies and theater teacher, where children continuously teach him the merits of patience. He is the Resident Artist at the New Classics Company theater in Hyannis, where he has written three plays and directed two. He is incredibly grateful to NWT for this opportunity, and hopes that the spark of new theatre continues to be flamed in NH.

K. M. Sorenson, a native of Lowell, Massachusetts, has had plays produced across the United States, including Gallery Players, Actors Studio of Newburyport, Boston Theater Marathon, Image Theater, Arlington Friends of the Drama, Footlight Club, Playwrights' Platform, Centastage, Firehouse Center for the Arts, ACME Theatre Productions, Shelterbelt Theater, Towne Street Theater, Lakeshore Players, Astor Street Opera Company, and Dubuque Fine Arts Players. Sorenson has been the moderator of Merrimack Valley Playwrights (www.mvplaywrights.com) since 2013.

Ellen Davis Sullivan's plays have been on stage in theaters across the country including in The Boston Theatre Marathon, at The Indie Boots Festival in Chicago, and in The Thalia Festival in New York City. Her one-act play Recessed! Or When the Mortgage Goes Upside Down was a winner of the Vermont Actors' Repertory Theater 2013 Nor-Eastern Playwrights' Competition. Ellen is an award-winning author of fiction whose stories have appeared in journals in print and online including Clarion, Stonecoast Review and Moment Magazine. Her essay "The Perfect Height for Kissing," won the 2014 Columbia Nonfiction Prize and is published in Issue 53 of Columbia: A Journal of Literature and Art. Ellen's plays have been published by Smith and Kraus, Applause Books and in Ponder Review. She is a member of the Dramatists' Guild.

Donald Tongue is a playwright with four published plays to his credit. His most produced work, *Void*, has been produced in Boston and Los Angeles. *School Portrait Monologues* was produced in New Zealand. *Fishbowl* was part of the 2010 short play festival in New York City at the Manhattan Repertory Theatre, where it was held over for an extended run. *My Neighbor, the Poet*, a play about Robert Frost, was commissioned and produced by theatre KAPOW in October 2010. *Scene Changes* was a featured work in the Page to Stage Encore production, Concord NH, produced at the Firehouse Center for the Arts 2012 New Works Festival, Newburyport MA, and produced at the Leddy Center for their 2015 Showcase Production series. *Candid Candidate* was produced at the Leddy Center for their 2016 Showcase Production series, and was later produced in October 2016 at the Hatbox Theatre. *The Truth Will Spring Yuh* was produced at the 2014 NHCTA Festival, Concord NH, and received its premiere full production in April 2017 at the Hatbox Theatre. Donald is a member of the Dramatists Guild of America, and founder and Managing Director of New World Theater.

APPENDIX B - PLAYWRIGHT CONTACT INFO

AMY OESTREICHER

Connecticut

amyoes70@gmail.com

(203) 209-4948

ANDREA APTECKER

Massachusetts

aptecker@yahoo.com

(617) 981-0868

ANDREA FLECK CLARDY

Massachusetts

afleckclardy@gmail.com

(617) 435-1521

CYNTHIA FAITH ARSENAULT

Massachusetts

cynthiafaith@comcast.net

(978) 828-8232

DON COHEN

Massachusetts

doncohen@rcn.com

(781) 863-1279

DONALD TONGUE

New Hampshire

donald@donaldtongue.com

(603) 264-4041

ELLEN DAVIS SULLIVAN

Massachusetts

LNDSullivan@comcast.net

(978) 470-2014

ERICA FURGIUELE

Vermont

erica.l.furgiuele@gmail.com

(215) 378-5442

EUGENIE CARABATSOS

New Hampshire

ecarabatsos@gmail.com

eugeniecarabatsos.com

GREG HOVANESIAN

Massachusetts

greghovanesian@gmail.com

(617) 872-6840

https://www.facebook.com/yabirdproductions/

GREG PARKER

New Hampshire

iamgumpus@gmail.com

(603) 499-1336

JAMES CELENZA

Rhode Island

jascelenza@gmail.com

(401) 351-5875

JOHN MINIGAN

Massachusetts

john.a.minigan@gmail.com

(508) 877-3302

K. M. SORENSON

Massachusetts

kmsorenson@hotmail.com

(978) 459-5150

LAWRENCE KESSENICH

Massachusetts

lkessenich50@gmail.com

(617) 281-8874

PATRICK GABRIDGE

Massachusetts

pat@gabridge.com

(617) 959-1437

SHARI D. FROST

Massachusetts

sharidfrost@icloud.com

(781) 816-3191

TOM COASH

Connecticut

Thomascoash@sbcglobal.net

(203) 645-5599

NEW WORLD THEATRE

Londonderry, NH

newworldtheatre.org

(603) 264-4041

literary@newworldtheatre.org

Made in United States
North Haven, CT
23 January 2025

64795631R00049